A Lullaby of Love for

Dean

By Suzanne Marshall

LiveWellMedia.com

ISBN-13: 978-1717176059
ISBN-10: 1717176054

This book is dedicated to

DEAN

who is loved very much!

Dean,

are you ready to give thanks tonight
for all that is peaceful, warm and bright?

Dean,

as the Deer plays guitar with glee,
we give thanks for you and me,
and our time together in harmony.

I AM
THANKFUL

Dean,

as the Hippo plays the violin,

we give thanks for giggles and grins,

and belly laughs from deep within.

Dean,

as the Owl drums like a pro,
we give thanks for adventures
that help us grow,
even "oopsy-daisies"
and "uh-ohs."

Dean,

as the Giraffe softly sings,

we give thanks for everything,

like smooches from pooches,

and butterfly wings.

Dean,

as the Eagle plays the harp,
we give thanks for your big heart;
you are brave and you are smart.

Dean,

as the Badger plays clarinet,

we give thanks for every breath,

like each deep breath

that helps us rest.

Dean,

as the Antelope plays maracas,

we give thanks for cuddles and hugs,

and all that is cozy,

comfy and snug.

Dean,

as the Elk plays the cello,

we give thanks that you are mellow,

like a spongy, sweet marshmallow.

Dean,

as the Bunny plays the violin,

we give thanks for family and friends,

and love that never,

ever ends.

Dean,

as the Fox plays the flute,

I give thanks that you are YOU.

You are loved and loving too.

Dean,

as the Bear plays the sax,

as you sleep, as you relax,

I LOVE YOU

to the moon and back.

GOODNIGHT
DEAN

Credits

Special thanks to my family and to my dear friends Hannah and Rachel Roeder. All illustrations have been edited by the author. Musical animals and hot-air balloon: © ddraw (freepik). Main cat, cat friend & sleeping kitty: © dazdraperma (fotosearch). Puppy: yayayoyo (fotosearch). Moon and lantern: © zzve (fotosearch). Floral ladder: © colematt (fotosearch). Additional elements were curated from freepik.

About the Author

An honors graduate of Smith College, Suzanne Marshall writes to inspire, engage and empower children. Learn more about Suzanne and her books at **LiveWellMedia.com**. *(Photo: Suzanne & Abby Underdog)*

More Personalized Books from LiveWellMedia.com

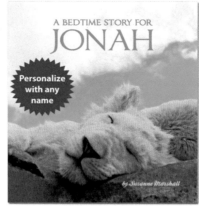

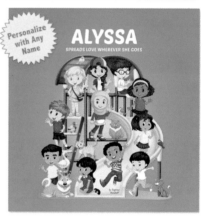

Made in the USA
Monee, IL
21 April 2022

95130736R00021